Quentin Blake

SNUFF

RED FOX

Some other books by Quentin Blake

All Join In
Angel Pavement
Angelo
Clown
Cockatoos
Fantastic Daisy Artichoke
The Green Ship
Loveykins
Mister Magnolia
Mrs Armitage and the Big Wave
Mrs Armitage on Wheels
Mrs Armitage Queen of the Road
Patrick
Quentin Blake's ABC
A Sailing Boat in the Sky
Simpkin
Zagazoo

SNUFF
A RED FOX BOOK 978 1 849 41048 9

First published in Great Britain by Jonathan Cape,
an imprint of Random House Children's Books
A Random House Group Company

Jonathan Cape edition published 1973
Red Fox edition published 2010

1 3 5 7 9 10 8 6 4 2

Red Fox Books are published by Random House Children's Books,
61–63 Uxbridge Road, London W5 5SA

www.kidsatrandomhouse.co.uk
www.rbooks.co.uk

Addresses for companies within The Random House Group Limited can be found at:
www.randomhouse.co.uk/offices.htm

THE RANDOM HOUSE GROUP Limited Reg. No. 954009

A CIP catalogue record for this book is available from the British Library.

Printed in China

One morning in early summer, many years ago, Sir Thomas Magpie was getting out of bed. He was unhappy because he'd just found that, in the night, the mice had been eating his boots again.

"Snuff!" he shouted. "SNUFF!"

Who was Snuff?

Snuff was Sir Thomas Magpie's page. A page is a boy who goes to live with a knight as his servant and also to learn how to be a knight himself when he grows up. Snuff very much wanted to be a knight but, unfortunately, although he tried his best, he didn't always get things right.

Snuff was sitting on the roof in the sunshine, feeding the pigeons. As he scattered the crumbs his mind was far away, imagining what it was like to be a knight and have all kinds of adventures.

When Snuff heard Sir Thomas calling he ran down to help him. First of all he brushed Sir Thomas's cloak for him. Then he got out a lot of hats so that Sir Thomas could decide which one to wear. And when Sir Thomas wasn't looking, Snuff tried one on himself to see how he would look when he became a knight.

Then, after breakfast in the great kitchen, Snuff tried his best to patch up Sir Thomas's boots while Mrs Posset, the housekeeper, made sandwiches for their lunch. Sir Thomas was feeling more cheerful now. He bounced around the kitchen telling exciting stories about famous knights and their battles with villains. Snuff got so carried away with these wonderful adventures that he made a very poor job of mending the boots.

Since it was a sunny day Sir Thomas was going to give Snuff his lessons on How to be a Knight out of doors. Soon they were both on Sir Thomas's horse, Flapdragon, and as they rode across the meadows and through the woods, they waved a cheery "Good morning" to all the countryfolk they met. A proper page should really have a horse of his own, but because Sir Thomas was poor and could only afford one horse (and even he was rather bony), Snuff had to ride behind.

They reached their favourite place by the bridge over the river, and started off with How to Hold a Sword, and Sword Fights.

But Snuff was so excited at the thought of being a Knight that he waved his sword too high and got it caught in the branches of a tree.

After that they had Dancing.

Snuff took three paces to the left when he should have taken three paces to the right, and put his foot in the sandwiches.

And then they had How to Bow.
     But Snuff bent over too quickly, lost
his balance, and tumbled backwards
into the river.

Sir Thomas gave a sigh as he wrung the water out of Snuff's clothes. "Snuff," he said, "at this rate it will be a very long time before we make a knight out of you."

"You can't sword-fight, you can't dance, you can't bow. And what's more, you can't even mend a pair of mouse-eaten boots." He pointed to his boots, which were now coming apart again. "It's no good," he said. "We'll have to pay a visit to the Bootmaker who lives in the clearing. On your feet, Snuff!"

So off they trotted through the woods. When they got near the Bootmaker's cottage, Sir Thomas and Snuff saw something very strange. Four ragged men were running like scarecrows from the cottage and cackling wickedly. Each of them was carrying an armful of boots.

When Sir Thomas and Snuff arrived at the cottage, they found the Bootmaker sitting on the front steps, with his head in his hands. "Oh dear," he moaned. "The four horrible Boot Thieves have just been here. And what's worse, they've threatened to come back with a cart and take away *all* my beautiful boots! Months and months of hard work wasted!"

The Bootmaker took Sir Thomas and Snuff down into his workshop in the cellar and there they saw rows and rows of his fine boots.

Sir Thomas waved his sword in the air angrily. "Steal your boots!" he shouted. "Just let them try!"

But the Bootmaker sighed sadly. "There are four of them," he said. "Four big, tough men. And there are only two and a half of us."

While the Bootmaker was talking, Snuff looked along the rows and rows of boots – ankle boots, calf boots, knee-length boots, thigh boots, in all shapes and colours and sizes – and suddenly he had an idea.

"Here, take these," he cried, and crammed as many boots as he could into the arms of Sir Thomas and the Bootmaker. "We're only just in time." They could hear a cart lumbering up to the cottage as they scrambled out by the back door.

Only a moment after, the four horrible Boot Thieves burst through the cellar door and down the steps with whoops of evil glee. "Just look at all these boots!" they chuckled, and rushed to try some on.

Suddenly, they stopped short in amazement.

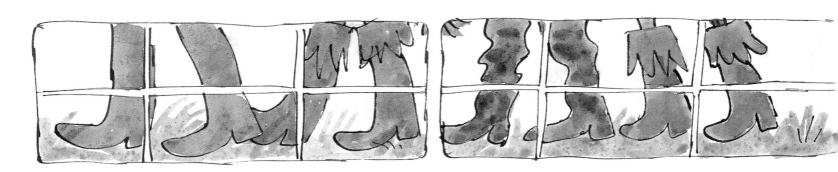

Outside, past the long narrow cellar window, tramped eight pairs of big feet: clump, clump, clump.

And they heard shouts of "Where are these famous Boot Thieves then?" and "Just let me get at them!" and "We'll teach them to steal other people's boots!"

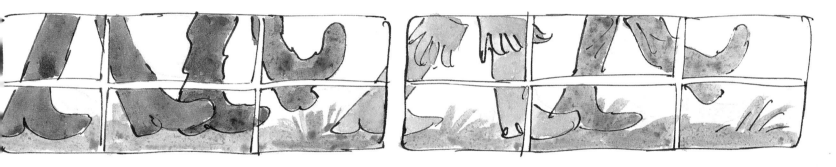

After that, eight more pairs of feet passed the window in the other direction: clump, clump, clump. There were shouts of "We'll go round this way and surprise them!" and "There are only four of them!" and "We'll make them squeal!"

Backwards and forwards they clumped, more and more and more feet, in boots of all shapes and sizes.

The Chief Boot Thief turned white with terror, because all
Boot Thieves are cowards, really. "W-w-we're outnumbered,"
he stammered. "Qu-qu-quick! Let's get out of here before they
catch us!"

And not even stopping to pick up their own boots, the four horrible Boot Thieves rushed off screaming into the woods, and were never seen again.

"What a clever idea, Snuff," said the Bootmaker, "for us all to put boots on our hands and feet, and keep walking backwards and forwards past the window." "Yes, indeed, Snuff," Sir Thomas agreed. And then they trotted around for a while on all fours, clump, clump, clump, just to show how happy they were. After that they all sat down and ate the sandwiches Mrs Posset had made that morning.

"Now it's my turn to do something for you," said the Bootmaker. "Boots for life! Whenever either of you wants a pair of boots, you have only to come to me and ask for them. In fact, I can see you both need new ones straight away!" Sir Thomas and Snuff were delighted and they began trying on boots there and then.

And that wasn't all. When Snuff had got his new boots on, the Bootmaker said, "Now come with me." They went to the orchard at the back of his house and there saw a little horse looking over a gate. "His name is Flinders," said the Bootmaker, "and I want you to have him, Snuff, so that you can learn to be a knight properly."

And so, when the sun was just beginning to set and it was time to say goodbye, Sir Thomas mounted Flapdragon and Snuff followed him on Flinders and together they rode off home.

"Well done, Snuff," said Sir Thomas. "I can see that you're going to be a first-rate knight after all!"

You can just imagine how pleased Snuff felt.